HARPER **Chapters**

BOOK #1

WEDNESDAY & WOOF

CATASTROPHE

By **SHERRI WINSTON**

Illustrated by
GLADYS JOSE

HARPER

An Imprint of HarperCollins*Publishers*

TO ALL THE LITTLE DETECTIVES.
KEEP SEARCHING, AND DREAMING,
AND BELIEVING.

Wednesday and Woof #1: Catastrophe

Library of Congress Control Number: 2020942276
ISBN 978-0-06-297601-7 — ISBN 978-0-06-297599-7 (pbk.)

Typography by Alice Wang
21 22 23 24 25   RTLO   10 9 8 7 6 5 4 3 2 1

First Edition

TABLE of CONTENTS

TIPS FOR BEING
A GOOD DETECTIVE

- Observe. Pay close attention. Everything could be a clue!

- Assess the situation—try to understand what is going on.

- Ask questions. What happened? When? Who was hurt or in trouble? Are there witnesses?

- Try not to jump to conclusions.

- Use your instincts. Trust your gut!"

CHAPTER #1
LOOKING FOR TROUBLE

"HEY, WOOF, do you see what I see?"

"Woof!" answers my dog, wagging his tail.

I look out from our boat office. It used to be a *boating* boat till grandpa retired and bought a new fishing boat. Now it sits in our backyard, where me and Woof get to use it as our headquarters.

We're detectives: the Wednesday and Woof Detective Agency, at your service. My name is Wednesday Walia Nadir.

My family calls me Walia, but I go by Wednesday when I'm on the job. Wednesday has always been my lucky day. I brought Woof home on a Wednesday!

I've got my binoculars glued to my eyeballs. Woof is standing at alert, taking long, deep breaths—sniffing out people in trouble.

"Look, Woof!" I point to three boys from my school who are walking across the street from my house. Older boys, maybe even fourth grade. They don't live around here.

Woof draws in another big whiff of air and *puff-puff-puff* blows it out. "You see it too, right, Woof?" He nods, his body rigid and on high alert.

Using skills learned from *The Big Book of Detective Tips*, I observe the boys.

WEDNESDAY & WOOF
DETECTIVE AGENCY

- They're looking over their shoulders.
- They seem fidgety.
- Something in my gut—that feeling you get deep down in your stomach—is telling me to keep an eye on those three.

I write my observations down in my detective notebook in case they become important.

Being observant is just one of the skills detectives need. We need to be able to gather information, too.

"Woof, let's get closer to the boys and look for more clues."

"Woof!" he says, agreeing with me.

I slip the honorary badge Aunt Nalia gave me into my pocket. She's a detective right here in Blossom County, Michigan. For now, I'm just in charge of my neighborhood, Blossom Heights.

Next, I stuff the pockets of Woof's support vest with the detective supplies we may need: a magnifying glass, the map I drew of our neighborhood, my notepad, and a pencil.

I place Woof's special support-dog vest on him and secure it. His vest lets people know he's working so they don't bother him.

Stealthily, Woof and I tiptoe down the steps that were built specially for me, with wider steps and solid railings.

WEDNESDAY AND WOOF DETECTIVE AGENCY

Daddy is in the yard filling the bird feeders. Blossom Lake is behind our house. It's so beautiful. I love how the little waves lap against the boat ramp. Thanks to the lake, our backyard has more birds and shade trees than the park.

It's all very soothing—unless you're on the hunt for mysteries to solve.

Woof and I creep closer . . . closer. Woof gives me a look and I nod. "You're right,

"Do you know who this Ollie is, Woof?" I ask. "Is he from this neighborhood?" I check in with my gut. It's telling me those boys are up to no good, but my detective book also says not to jump to conclusions.

Being a detective is hard work!

I want to rush over and demand they tell me what they're up to when...a shriek pierces the calm morning and jangles my nerves. A cry for help!

Someone needs us— RIGHT NOW!

YOU'VE READ ONE CHAPTER! THAT'S OVER 700 WORDS!

Woof. We need to take cover!" I scoot over to a large French lilac bush that edges our side yard. We peer between leaves. I can see Mrs. Winters's house across the street. The boys are on the sidewalk.

". . . get Ollie," I hear the thin boy say. The one in the hat adds, "Gnarly. Ollie is, like, the dude. I'm in as long as we don't get caught!"

Don't get caught! Hmm . . . that sounds like a clue.

The boys are definitely up to something.

CHAPTER #2

WHEN DANGER CALLS . . .

"**WALIA AND** Woof, I need you!" Our neighbor, Mrs. Winters, is running toward us. "It's Autumn! She's run away, and if we don't find her soon, she and I will miss our vacation. *Ohhh!*" she says in her singsongy voice.

Woof wrinkles his brow and steps back. Our neighbor lady can be a little loud.

"Woof," I whisper, "it's a real mystery. And a serious one, too."

Autumn is a sweet little indoor kitty who belonged to Grandpa, but Mrs. Winters takes care of her now.

Mrs. Winters sings, "Wednesdaaay!" She is a very fancy lady with glossy hair that's high and tall. Lips shiny and pink. Clothes that sparkle and shine.

And she sings—a lot! Not regular songs. Her songs are Italian. She calls her special singing "opera." Me and Woof call it loud. Woof looks like he wants to cover his ears.

My mind races. I need to ask questions, come up with a plan for this investigation. If Autumn is out there, we'll find her.

Just then, Daddy comes over carrying a tray of flowers. He says, "Good morning, Mrs. Winters. Is there a problem?"

Uh-oh. My parents are very protective because I have something called juvenile arthritis. If he thinks the mission is too much for me, it could be a whole other kind of trouble.

I hold my breath, waiting.

But I don't want to be calm. I want to take off!

Woof nudges me, reminding me to be cool. I take a deep breath and explain what's going on. Why me and Woof have to find Autumn. I leave out my suspicions about the strange big kids.

I don't want Mrs. Winters to sing any songs of despair.

Daddy kneels and sets the tray of brightly colored pansies on the grass beside me. Shadows from all the trees dance across his face. He places his other hand on my shoulder. "Walia, I think it's great that you want to help, but . . ."

No! No! No! Not the BIG BUT. I hate the BIG BUT!

Whenever grown-ups want to stop you from doing something, they pretend to listen, and then they hit you with the BIG BUT.

"I'll be fine, Daddy. Really! I've got Woof to help me!" I say. Wide smile. Puppy dog eyes—mine and Woof's. Most grown-ups would melt at this show of utter sincerity, but my daddy shakes his head.

13

"Walia Nadir, you know you have to respect your body. What if you get another fever? Remember how tired you were and how much pain you were in? And it's only been a few months since we've gotten your symptoms under control."

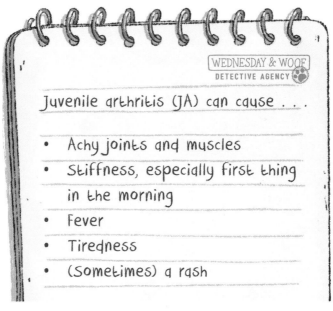

WEDNESDAY & WOOF
DETECTIVE AGENCY

Juvenile arthritis (JA) can cause . . .

- Achy joints and muscles
- Stiffness, especially first thing in the morning
- Fever
- Tiredness
- (Sometimes) a rash

"But Daddy, what's the point of being healthy and safe if I get bored to death?"

He sighs, a very Daddy thing to do.

Grandpa never treats me like a sick person. He always tells me, "You can be anything you want, Walia, no matter the challenges!" I like that. And it's true. I'm not going to let a challenge like JA get the best of me.

"Daddy!" I place my hand on his shoulder. "I won't overdo it, promise. Please may I go now and find sweet, precious, helpless little Autumn?"

Daddy laughs and shakes his head at me.

"Just make sure 'being on the case' doesn't wear you out. Woof has been trained as a support dog—lean on him when you need to."

"*Wednesdaaay!*" Mrs. Winters sings. Even though her singing hurts my ears, an idea hits me with a wallop. I gasp!

Woof tilts his head toward me while Daddy is still fussing. I whisper, "I have an idea!"

MRS. WINTERS is leading us to the scene of the crime when a familiar bark makes the hairs on my arms tickle.

"Gruff! Gruff! Gruff!" I look at Woof. He looks at me. We know that bark—it's the dog of my biggest rival and school bossy pants, Anita B. Moosier.

Me and Woof pick up our pace until we're safely inside Mrs. Winters's backyard. Away from bossy Anita B. and her equally bossy dog!

"This is Autumn's favorite spot in my yard," says Mrs. Winters. She waves her hand at a shady clump of grass near a tree. "She's mostly an indoor cat, you know?"

I do know. Autumn cat lived with Grandpa and us until we figured out that Raafe, my twin brother, was a little allergic. Now she lives with Mrs. Winters, but me and Grandpa still get to visit.

Mrs. Winters points to the house and an open window. "Usually, if she leaves her special perch in the window, Autumn will come out here and take a nap," she says, "but only when it's shady. She doesn't like too much sun, and she isn't a fan of all the noise in the park, either."

"Please tell us everything you remember," I say, pulling out my pad and pencil.

Woof sits by my side, ready to listen.

Woof has a perfect memory, but I need to take notes. Mrs. Winters says she saw the cat hop onto the lawn and cozy up to her favorite spot, but when Mrs. Winters looked out her window again, Autumn was gone.

"And she was wearing her favorite diamond-studded red collar. I had the diamonds removed from one of my old tiaras," she says.

I try not to let my eyes go *boing* out of my head. A missing cat. A diamond cat collar.

Is it possible Autumn isn't just lost? Maybe someone took her!

"Is the collar worth a lot of money?" I ask. I'm holding on to the pencil so hard, it slips from my fingers. Woof scoops it up with his teeth and waits for me to take it back.

Mrs. Winters twists her lips to one side like she's thinking hard. She says, "A lot of money? I suppose so, but what does that matter? It's Autumn I'm concerned about!"

Woof and I exchange looks. Mrs. Winters doesn't get it.

CLUES

- Strange boys hanging out near Mrs. Winters's house

- Autumn is wearing a fancy, expensive diamond collar

- CONCLUSION—Maybe the boys are . . . diamond thieves?

- But what would a bunch of fourth grade boys know about diamonds?

- Need more clues!

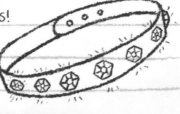

Could the boys really be diamond thieves? Or worse—*catnappers*? I almost tell Mrs. Winters what I'm thinking, except Woof says it's not a good idea. Well, he doesn't say it out loud, but I can tell what he's thinking.

Mrs. Winters dabs her eyes with a tissue. Her long, black eyelashes quiver like spider legs. Woof looks afraid. He does not like spiders or quivery black eyelashes that look like spiders. I scratch behind his ears to calm him down.

Mrs. Winters tosses her arm over her face. Ah, yes. The pose of despair. You see that a lot in our line of work. Woof and I have been solving mysteries for a long, long time—almost two whole months. We've seen it all!

"What else can you tell us?" I ask. Woof pays close attention.

A good detective asks the right questions.

"What else does Autumn like to do?" I ask.

WEDNESDAY & WOOF
DETECTIVE AGENCY

A few facts about
Autumn. She loves:

- Lying in the shade
- Watching birds play
- Listening to the sound of the
  lake waves lapping the shore
- Eating warm bread from the
  bakery
- Being in a peaceful place

"Oh my!" Mrs. Winters wails. "My beautiful kitty didn't even have breakfast. I'll bet she's so hungry. You must find her!"

"Why didn't she eat?" I ask.

Mrs. Winters bats her spidery lashes. "She was too excited about our trip!" she says.

Woof is already sniffing the air.

Sniff-sniff-sniff!

He has the best nose in town. While he sniffs, I observe.

My eyes go zoom-zoom-zoom over the blades of grass.

I look for anything out of the ordinary.

Anything that does not belong.

Just then, Woof lets out a sharp *"Woof!"*

I know what that bark means. That's his I-found-a-clue bark.

My eyes continue to zoom-zoom-zoom. Then I see it, too!

CHAPTER #4

CATNAPPERS!

"FOLLOW THAT sparkle!" I say.

Woof agrees.

He uses his nose and points at a shiny object.

"Look, Woof!" I start to bend, but Woof nudges the object with his nose. He pushes it up, up, up against the huge rock beside the sidewalk. The higher he gets it, the less I have to bend.

"Thanks, Woof," I say, reaching for the shiny object. It's a little damp from his nose but I don't mind. "It's . . . a diamond stud. Same as what Mrs. Winters described. Woof, this is a great clue!"

"Woof!" he barks, and wags his tail. Then he's on alert. When he barks again, he dips his head. He points with his nose to a trail of paw prints.

When I show Mrs. Winters the diamond stud, she gasps. "Oh my! That came off my little darling's collar!"

"Don't worry, we'll find her soon!" We follow the curving sidewalk around the gate and along the road.

We pause. Woof sniffs the air.
Sniff-sniff-sniff.

Then he sniffs the ground. I shove my notepad back inside Woof's vest pocket and take out my magnifying glass. I bend down for a closer look. Hmm! Tiny footprints in the soft, dark earth of the flower bed. Not footprints. Paw prints.

"Let's go!" I say. Excitement tickles my skin and gives me a zing!

This is way better than the time we helped old Mrs. Harris find her house shoes (under her couch) or Mom find her new paint-brushes (in her closet).

Excitement grows with each step. Auntie Nalia taught me to pay attention because one clue will lead to the next, then the next, and soon you've solved a crime.

It doesn't take long before I find two more diamond studs. Woof helps me pick them up.

Then he points his nose at the ground and shows me another clue.

"The paw prints are all gone?" I say. Why do they just seem to vanish? Then I remember the boys, and I think of something I hadn't remembered. Skateboards. The boys all had skateboards.

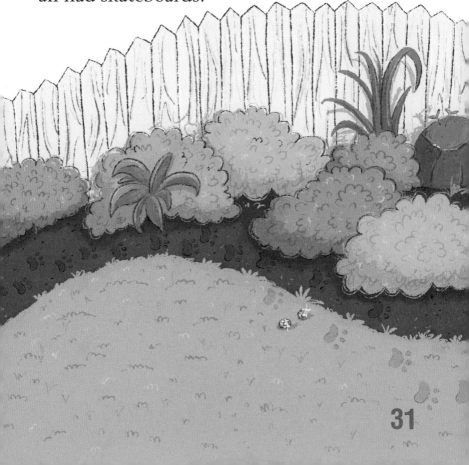

31

I'm about to share my clue with Woof when I notice he's following his own clue.

He growls low. I look up just in time to see them—the three boys! They are racing across the street—all riding skateboards.

And underneath the tall, thin boy's arm is something small, white, and fluffy!

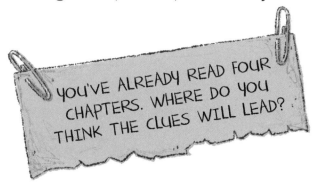

YOU'VE ALREADY READ FOUR CHAPTERS. WHERE DO YOU THINK THE CLUES WILL LEAD?

CHAPTER #5
THEY'RE GETTING AWAY!

ZOOM! ZOOM! Zoom!

The boys quickly vanish around the next corner. Where are they going? How will I ever catch them? Is Autumn okay?

"Good boy," I say to Woof. He wags his tail. I almost lean in for a nuzzle, but when he's working, he's all business. Instead, I tickle his ears and say, "Time to work!"

Woof turns so that the pockets of his vest face me. I remove my map from a vest pocket.

Then I lean on Woof's back until I'm sitting on the ground. I'm not hurting at all today, but Daddy says you can't be too careful.

I spread the map out on the ground. Our neighborhood is shaped like a circle.

I squint at the big hill. They were sort of

headed in that direction. On this side, the hill is grassy with trees. On the other side, there's a path that leads to a strip of concrete.

Three boys with skateboards.

A secluded area of Blossom Park.

A quiet hill.

And a missing fancy cat.

"Woof, I think they're heading over there." I point to a hill about . . . two blocks away. "Let's follow them."

Woof lets out a gentle bark.

"Trust me, Woof, Daddy is overprotecting me," I say. Three months ago the doctors worked to figure out why my fever wouldn't go away. My legs felt heavy and achy. I had a rash, too. Finding out about my JA was good because they knew how to fix it. I feel better now. Remembering makes me chew my lip.

Woof nuzzles me even though he's on duty. I've only had him two months, but he already knows how much I don't like to be babied.

"Okay, Woof," I say, determined not to give up, "we'll head in that direction. But we'll go kinda slow." He licks my face and wags his tail. I'm feeling really good, then all the good feelings shrivel up and die. Two shadows spring up behind me and Woof like stinkweed in a garden.

With a big eye roll and a heavy sigh, I turn. I say, "Hello, Anita B. Moosier."

CHAPTER #6

BUNNY POWER!

"I'VE TOLD you a thousand times!" says Anita B. "It's pronounced Moose-E-A, like the French!"

Like I care. I fold my arms and stare at her and her bully bulldog, Gruff. That dog is mean as a snake, but she likes poor Woof. Now she's trying to sniff him, and he's getting that low growl in his chest that means *don't mess with me.*

"Anita B. Moosey-Goose, call off your dog,

please. Woof doesn't want her dog breath all over him. Besides, he's wearing his vest, which means he's working."

She pooches out her lips in her Anita B. way and says, "Oh, I forgot, your dog is here because he has to be. It's his *job*."

"You take that back!" I say.

"Woof!" says my dog in a low, protective bark.

Anita B. makes an eeky squealing sound. "Don't bite my head off!" Then in a sugary sweet voice, she adds, "Anyway, we have to go. Me and *my* dog are going to the park to go bike riding with friends."

"Since when does your dog know how to ride a bike?" I ask.

"You know exactly what I mean, *Detective Wednesday.*"

Of all the neighborhoods in the world, why does Anita B. live in mine?

WEDNESDAY & WOOF
DETECTIVE AGENCY

Things I hate the most EVER!
- Bullies
- Anybody who baby talks to me. yuck!
- Anyone who tries to rub my juvenile arthritis in my face by telling me stuff like they're going bike riding. Oh brother!

"My mom says I'm supposed to be nice to you and watch out for you in case you need help," she says in her mean-baby voice. "Even when you're pretending to be a detective."

"I'm not pretending!" I say. "I am a *real* detective with a real case to solve over the hill!"

She starts to circle around me the same way Gruff does Woof. My dog is on work alert. He doesn't move. Good thing, because Anita B.'s making me dizzy. Is she going to start sniffing me, too?

Luckily, I don't have to find out because my best friend hop-hop-hops in between me and Anita B.

"Beat it, Belinda Bundy!" snarls Anita B. "Nobody invited you!"

I look at my best friend, Belinda Bundy, and smile. Belinda likes dressing like a bunny and Anita B. Moosey-Goose hates it when she does.

So Belinda hops around and around and around Anita B. and Gruff. I make a buck-toothed bunny rabbit face and begin hopping too—gently, of course. I try to make my imaginary whiskers pop.

Then Belinda takes a carrot out of her pocket and starts chomping it. She offers me one, and I chomp, too.

"You two are both weirdos. Come on, Gruff. Let's get out of here!"

Anita B. says. Then she pauses and gets her sickening sweet look and says, "If I were you, I wouldn't even try climbing that hill. You might not be strong enough, *Detective Wednesday*!"

She prances away and I shake my head.

"Woof!" says my dog, giving them a hearty farewell. Belinda gives me a high five, and we fall into the grass laughing.

It feels good to laugh, but then I remember what I was doing. I sit up on the edge of the lawn, my eyes wide.

"Belinda, I'm pretty sure they went up the hill. Three older boys who are the prime suspects. I think they might have Autumn."

44

"Oh no!" says Belinda. "What can we do?"

I think about it for a second. Part of me wonders, *What if Anita B. is right? What if I can't make it up the hill?* Woof moves closer to me, letting me know I have his support. Woof is right. I'm not going to let a challenge like JA get the best of me. Besides, sometimes slowing down gives me more time to pick up clues other detectives might not see.

"We have to go after them," I say. "Before they get away!"

CHAPTER #7
THE CAT'S OUT OF THE BAG!

I TELL Belinda about the boys I spotted earlier and how Mrs. Winters came over and asked me and Woof to please find Autumn.

"We followed a trail of these jewels," I say, showing Belinda the diamond studs I had tucked into Woof's vest. "That's when we saw the same boys we'd spotted lurking around earlier. They were speeding away on their skateboards, carrying something small, white, and fluffy under one of their arms."

Belinda Bundy gasps. "Those look like real diamonds."

"They are," I say. "Mrs. Winters says so."

Then she chews her lip and says, "Remember, Walia, just because you saw the boys hanging around, it doesn't mean they have Autumn."

I give a big sigh. Belinda Bundy is like that. Always trying to be mature. I have no time for maturity. I am trying to solve a mystery!

"Belinda, I saw them skateboarding over here like they were trying to hide something. And they were carrying a small, white, fluffy thing." I give her a wide-eyed look, meaning *Can't you see what I mean?*

When she says nothing, I continue. "I figured they were heading over to the hill. That's where we were going when Anita B. showed up."

Belinda gives it another few seconds of thought. Then she says, "I will go check it out with you, but you have to promise not to get too . . . too . . ."

"Too what?" Sometimes it's hard to be a girl of adventure and mystery-solving when your best friend is so cautious.

"Ahead of yourself. You know?" she says. "Jumping to conclusions. Rushing ahead no matter what."

I promise to try, but already I want to race fast like lightning. I start to run, but Woof weaves in front of me. He wants me to slow down. I don't want to slow down. But I don't want to wind up in the hospital again, either. The more we walk uphill, the harder it feels. A teeny-tiny ache itches the back of my leg. I bite my lip but don't say anything.

Woof senses something is wrong. He whines. I whisper, "I'm okay. Really!" Belinda is a little bit ahead, so she doesn't hear.

Once we reach the top of Beacon Hill, I let out a long breath. "You okay?" Belinda asks.

"I'm okay," I say. "Hey, what's that sound?"

A strange noise shushes through the trees. I motion for Belinda and Woof to stop. Woof climbs higher on the small, grassy hill and pokes his head through a cluster of bushes. He turns back to me and bobs his head up and down. He's a good support dog, but an *excellent* detective.

Belinda Bundy grabs hold of my hand and almost pulls me up the last few steps. I could've climbed it by myself, but I appreciate the help. Through the tall hedges, I see something that makes me let out a gasp!

"That's them!" I whisper. "The boys! And they've got girls with them, too!"

Then I see something propped up on the grass. One of their jackets almost hides it, but I can still see a little bit of a fluffy, white lump.

Autumn!

"I bet they're filming a ransom video!" I say.

"Or maybe they're just filming each other doing skateboard stunts," Belinda says. I try not to sigh again, but she really isn't seeing the big picture. They could be criminals.

Belinda laughs. "I know those boys!" she says.

I squint. "I'm sure I've seen them at our school, but I don't know them. What do you know about them? Any history of theft? Have they ever been involved in kidnapping?"

I think these are all excellent questions, but Belinda Bundy is shaking her head slowly back and forth.

"They're not like that," she says. "The tall, thin boy is Karen Gillespie's brother. And one of them is named Ryan. He goes to our church. He's not too bad for an older kid."

Hmph! Maybe she's right. But maybe . . .

I ease closer and closer to get a better view. Belinda must sense what I'm about to do, because she whispers, "No, Wednesday!" but I can't stop myself.

When I get close enough, I grab the white bundle. Soon as I tuck it under my arm, the boys look up.

"Hey! What're you doing?" asks the boy in the hat. "That's mine!"

"*Aha!*" I say. "Thought you'd get away with it, didn't you?"

But when I toss aside the grungy jacket in triumph, I'm the one who gets a big fat surprise!

SURPRISE? WHAT DO YOU THINK WEDNESDAY HAS FOUND?

CHAPTER #8
BACK TO BASICS

I'M EXPECTING our beautiful Autumn. Instead, a fuzzy white backpack opens and some kind of wheels tumble out.

"Hey!" the boys shout. "Those are ours. Give them back!" All of a sudden, the whole group of kids is rushing at me.

Gulp! They look mad.

Me and Belinda Bundy link arms. Woof moves in front of us and gives them his best guard-dog growl.

I'm secretly glad to have both of them on my side.

Grandpa likes to say, "The best defense is a good offense!" I'm never sure exactly what it means, but before they can get too close, I draw a deep breath, unlink my arm, and step around Woof.

"A cat is missing, and we're looking for it!" I say it in a loud voice that I hope sounds confident. The boys and two older girls stop, staring at us.

The boy with the hat says, "You lost your cat?" Funny. Up close he doesn't look anything like a robber or a kidnapper. He's just a boy with a little chocolate smeared on his face. Then I realize maybe they are from our neighborhood.

I tell them it's Mrs. Winters's cat and she's missing, and when I saw them racing by with something fluffy and white, I thought it might be Autumn.

"Oh! You poor thing," says one of the girls with a swoopy Afro. Both girls come over and give us pats on the shoulder. The tall, thin boy looks very serious.

"Gosh! We wouldn't ever do something like that. We like Mrs. Winters and her cat is cool."

One of the other boys says, "Yeah. That cat *is* cool. Very fancy, the way she prances around in the backyard."

Belinda Bundy gives my arm a squeeze. Woof glances up at me before sitting at my feet. It turns out the big kids aren't so strange. They're actually pretty nice.

"We wanted to come over here to skateboard while our parents are out doing Saturday errands," the boy in the hat says. They all nod.

I stoop to pick up the spilled wheels,

and a twinge of tightness squeezes around my knees. I frown but don't say anything. Twinges are one of the things that happen sometimes before my knee joints start to hurt. I hand over the wheels, saying, "Here you go. Hey, by the way, who is Ollie?"

A second goes by and everyone is quiet. Then the older kids all burst into laughter. Belinda Bundy looks at me and both of us shrug. Woof stands, walks around in a circle, and shakes his head. Even nice big kids can be weird.

"Little dudes," says the tall, skinny kid. "Ollie is a move we do on our skateboards. We're trying to get really good."

The girl with the Afro jumps in. "Yeah, that's why we have to sneak over here to practice! We live a few blocks over and have nowhere to skateboard."

We wave goodbye, and they wish us good luck before they head back up the hill to practice racing down. I reach inside Woof's vest and take out my notepad.

"What're you going to do now?" asks Belinda Bundy.

"It's time to get back to basics. I'm going to check my notes and think about the clues!" I pull out my map again, checking for possible places to search.

Belinda Bundy was right about the boys. They weren't involved. I guess when I saw them, my imagination got too excited and I jumped to conclusions. I won't make that mistake again.

Woof sniffs the air, and a small smile tugs at his mouth. He's onto something. I can always tell.

"I think I might be onto a clue, too."

Just then the wind picks up. It shakes the leaves in the trees. And snatches my map right out of my fingers!

"Woof!" barks my assistant.

"Run!" I shout. "Follow that map!"

CHAPTER 9

A CLUE IS IN THE AIR!

QUICKLY, WE chase the map toward Main Street. Belinda Bundy runs ahead of me. My legs are a little achy, but Woof is at my side and we're moving as fast as we can. We pass several houses before the map stops to rest on a patch of grass. Belinda and Woof beat me to it. I grab it and fold it, placing it back in the vest. Then I remove my notepad and reread a note.

A few facts about Autumn. She loves:

- Lying in the shade
- Watching birds play
- Listening to the sounds of the lake waves lapping the shore
- Eating warm bread from the bakery
- Being in a peaceful place

Woof tilts his nose in the air again and takes a deep, long sniff. He nods. So do I.

"What is it?" Belinda asks.

"Smell that?" I say. "It's bread. Fresh, *warm* bread. And there's only one place that's coming from."

"Señor Panadero's Bakery?" says Belinda Bundy.

"Exactly. Come on. Mrs. Winters told us Autumn left without eating," I say.

Belinda hops. I move gingerly, trying not to frown or chew my lip. The summer sunshine felt nice and silky this morning. Now it's starting to burn. Uh-oh. Another sign I might be wearing myself down. My JA makes me more sensitive to sunlight. I want to lie in a fountain to cool off. Woof trots alongside me. I force a smile. Everything will be fine. It will.

We round the corner onto Lighthouse Lane, and sure enough, there's Señor Panadero's truck, parked right in front of his shop.

"Señoritas, ¿cómo están? How are you?" He calls out his familiar greeting. I giggle like always. I like being a señorita! When we reach him, I feel a little winded.

"Autumn, Mrs. Winters's cat," I say, catching my breath. "Have you seen her?" Now Woof is winding his way around my body again—his signal for me to sit. I don't want anyone fussing over me. But Belinda hops into a sitting position and waves for me to do the same. I do, and Woof joins us.

Señor Panadero's round cheeks, rosy from the warmth of the sun and heat from his oven, lift into a wide grin. "Ah, Autumn. She is a fancy cat. A fancy cat for a fancy woman," he says.

"She ran off this morning," I say, "and if I can't find her soon, Mrs. Winters will have to cancel her vacation."

"Oh no!" he says. His bushy eyebrows shoot up. "And with your grandpa coming home today, too! I'm sure he'll want to see his fancy little cat, Miss Autumn."

"Grandpa?" I say with a gasp. Then I remember. Of course. He's been traveling all over with his new fishing boat, but he's coming home tonight. How could I forget? Now I've *really* got to find Autumn.

Belinda seems to sense my frustration. "Señor Panadero, have you seen her?" she asks.

"Why, yes! Yes, I have. Come. She was right over here in the shade." He leads us to a shady spot near his front door. Only with the sun climbing higher and higher in the sky, the spot isn't quite so shady.

"Well, my goodness! She was just here. And she was eating a hunk of my bread, too. Nice and warm, just how she likes it," he says.

My heart feels like it has fallen down an elevator.

I sigh. What's next? Just then, Woof begins pawing at a spot on the walkway that leads out the side gate. At first, I don't see anything. But when I take out my magnifying glass, I spot it.

Another jewel!

"She's leaving a trail again!" I say.

I'm so excited that I jump for joy, only to land and feel like a thousand needles are poking through my feet and legs.

"Ow!" I cry out, just before slumping to the ground!

ONLY TWO MORE CHAPTERS LEFT. YOU MUST LOVE MYSTERIES AS MUCH AS WEDNESDAY AND WOOF!

CHAPTER #10
PUTTING THE PIECES TOGETHER

"WOOF!" WOOF'S bark is loud and strong. Now he isn't asking me to rest. He's telling me to be still. He's also calling for help. Right then, we hear a familiar *whirr-whirr-whirr* sound. I realize it's Mr. Marshall on his official-business golf cart.

"You cowgirls look like you could use a hand," he says, tipping the brim of his hat toward us.

"Oh, thank goodness, Mr. Marshall. Poor Walia just crumpled," Señor Panadero says, wringing his hands.

"I'm fine," I say, trying to get up on my own. I hate when anyone calls me "poor Walia." Woof gets real close, and I clasp the harness on his vest. Slowly, as he moves forward, I feel the pressure lessen in my legs. "I'm not poor anything, just need to take a break," I say.

The magnifying glass is still in my hands. Despite my fall, I am able to see the shine of a white diamond mixed in with the bread-crumbs trailing the edge of the grass. Mr. Marshall, the security guard for our community, accepts a warm slice of breakfast bread. Señor Panadero says, "Wednesday, when you go home, tell your papá I'll be over soon with the bread he ordered for your abuelo."

I nod absently. I'm still eyeballing the thin trail of crumbs that leads to the curb.

"Wednesday, what now?" asks Belinda Bundy. Woof stands. I scratch under his chin and nuzzle his nose. I whisper to him that I know I need to slow down.

"Wouldn't mind at all giving you young ladies a ride on my motorized pony," says Mr. Marshall with a chuckle.

"Okay," I say, "but would you mind going kinda slow? See that trail of crumbs over there? I'd like to follow it. We're looking for Mrs. Winters's cat."

"Yes, sirree! Slow it is. Climb aboard!"

It isn't long before the trail of diamonds disappears about two houses down from mine. When we reach my house, I wave and say, "Thanks, Mr. Marshall. I think I can take it from here!" He touches the tip of his hat, just the way an old-fashioned cowboy might. Belinda tells me she has to hop back home for lunch.

"Let me know how it goes," she says. One of the bunny ears on her headband is bent. She hugs me gently, and I hug her back.

"I will. I promise."

I lean on Woof until we reach the bottom step of our front porch. I put my weight on him, and he eases me into a sitting position on the middle step. "Thanks, Woof," I say, kissing the top of his head.

"Woof!" He wags his tail, and I grab my notebook and pencil. I also pull out the map I drew of our neighborhood.

Sometimes the best way to solve a mystery is to review all the facts before jumping to a conclusion. Belinda was right. I do get carried away sometimes.

I take out my colored pencil and draw on the map everywhere we thought Autumn went.

We look at the facts we got from Mrs. Winters. My hands feel tired from so much writing and note-taking. Woof nudges the pages of my notebook with his shiny, black nose.

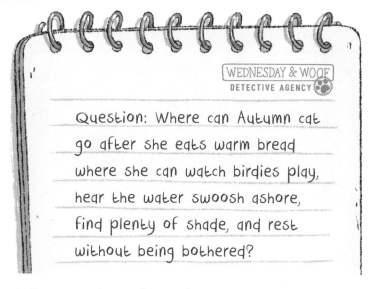

WEDNESDAY & WOOF
DETECTIVE AGENCY

Question: Where can Autumn cat go after she eats warm bread where she can watch birdies play, hear the water swoosh ashore, find plenty of shade, and rest without being bothered?

After reading for a few minutes, my eyes grow big.

"Woof," I say with a grin, "I know exactly where Autumn cat has to be!"

"DADDY, I think I solved our mystery!"

Daddy is holding another tray. This one is filled with petunias and marigolds. However, as soon as he sees me, he sets down the tray.

"Walia, you look tired. Do you need to rest?" he asks. I shake my head. It's hard to get anything past a dad. But I have to try.

"Brother, do not baby her so," says a voice. I turn to see my mom and Aunt Nalia walking toward us.

"Auntie!" I say. "I was just telling Daddy I think I've put all the clues together. I know the answer to the mystery!"

She smiles. "He told me you were on a case."

"She's overworked herself. Look at her. I can see the fatigue in her eyes!" says Daddy.

"Please, Daddy. I will rest, but just let me show you what I figured out!"

"Woof!" barks my protective dog.

I step carefully around the adults and head

for my boat office. "Please. Wait there!" I say. Woof is right where I need him to be. He pulls alongside me, and I lean into his soft, warm body as I climb the steps to the Wednesday and Woof headquarters.

Near the trees, the birdbath gurgles. The sun is becoming a bright yellow ball in the sky.

And tucked away in a cluster of shaded grass beneath the birdbath lies a soft lump of white fur.

She loves a shady place where she can listen to the waves lap against the shore, watch birds play, and nap without worrying about children in the park pulling her long, fluffy tail.

"Look!" I nudge Daddy, who followed me and Woof onto our boat office even though I asked him to wait. "After running around the neighborhood and dropping jewels and eating bread, she came to our house—her first home—to rest."

Daddy throws back his head and laughs. "It's the best patch of grass on Blossom Lake. But how did you figure it out?"

I show him my notebook. "It's right here in my detective notes. See?"

Daddy leans in close to take a look.

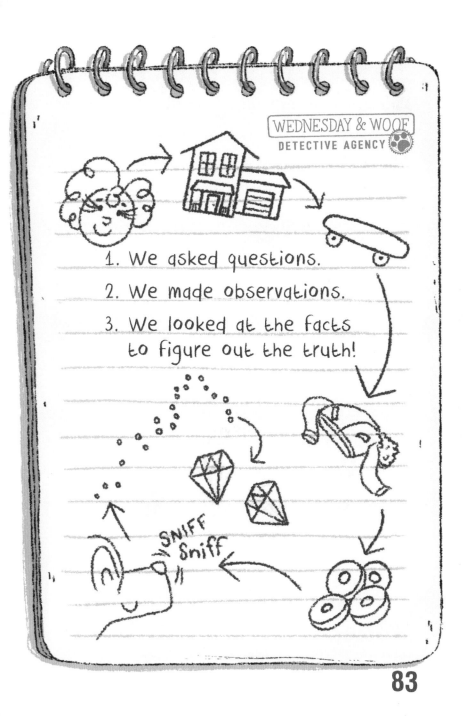

1. We asked questions.
2. We made observations.
3. We looked at the facts to figure out the truth!

SNIFF
Sniff

"I kinda messed up on this part," I tell Daddy, pointing to number three. I jumped to a few conclusions.

"And lastly, I used my instincts. Woof, too!"

Daddy hugs me and kisses the top of my head. "You're amazing, Walia Nadir—I mean Detectives Wednesday and Woof!"

We look up to see Mrs. Winters moving across the edge of our front lawn. "Look who I *fo-oooooo-und*!" she sings.

"Grandpa!" I squeal from the boat's deck. "Autumn was lost but we found her. The first official case of the Wednesday and Woof Detective Agency has been solved!"

"*Hoo-raaaaaaaaaaaaaaay!*" sings Mrs. Winters. Daddy goes and plucks the napping cat from her hiding spot. He hands her to Mrs. Winters. Mom and Auntie applaud.

"I knew you could do it," says Mom.

"Never doubted you!" calls Auntie.

Grandpa begins climbing the stairs, and all at once my eyes get drippy and I blurt, "I'm so happy I was able to find her. Anita B. said I wasn't strong enough to solve a real mystery and I was afraid if I couldn't solve it, I'd be a disappointment to Grandpa."

Grandpa frowns, charges up the last remaining steps, and then sweeps me into his arms. "My girl, you could never, ever, ever, disappoint me. You're my skipper!"

Daddy climbs up again and says, "Kiddo, as long as you're doing your best, you could never disappoint us. But we will discuss your need to take better care of yourself after you've rested. I can tell you're worn out."

"I love you, Daddy!" I say it brightly and sweetly. He is not amused.

Mrs. Winters hugs her cat and waves, saying, "You saved our vacation, Wednesday and Woof! We have just enough time to catch our plane. You are the best detectives!"

Daddy and Grandpa give each other a pat on the back. "Papa, would you care for some tea?" Daddy asks. Grandpa follows him down the steps and across the lawn. Both turn and wave, and Daddy tells me to come inside soon.

I drop onto a deck chair and stare out at the lake, leaning into Woof, and happy with our perfect day. "Woof, we did it!" I say.

I hold out my hand and Woof places his paw inside. We shake on it. I remove his vest and set it aside. Now he's off duty, and people can pet him and we can play together. Soon as I get a little rest.

It's gotten even warmer, but breezes off the water make it feel amazing.

"Woof, I think Autumn was right about this being the best spot in Blossom Heights for napping."

"Woof!" says the best dog in the world. "Woof! Woof!"

"You're right!" I say, tickling behind his ears.

All is calm for now, but just like Woof says, we never know where the next mystery will begin for the Wednesday and Woof Detective Agency!

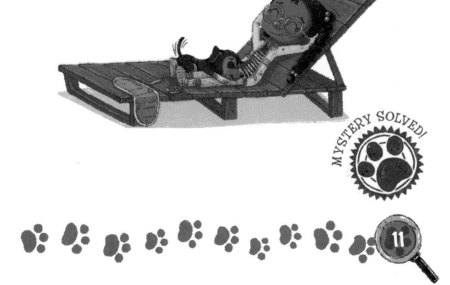

MYSTERY SOLVED!

CONGRATULATIONS!

You've read **11** chapters,

89 pages,

and **7,106** words!

What a *paw*-some effort!

FUN AND GAMES FOR DETECTIVES IN TRAINING

THINK

Making lists is one detective tool Wednesday uses to find Autumn. List five things about yourself that would make you a great detective!

SNIFF
Sniff

FEEL

In this book, Anita B. Moosier assumes Wednesday isn't strong because she has JA. Think of a time somebody believed something about you that wasn't true. How did that make you feel? Have you ever jumped to conclusions about someone else?

ACT

When Wednesday is on the hunt for a mystery, she starts by observing her neighborhood. Pick a friend or family member and write down everything you notice about them for five minutes.

My name is **SHERRI WINSTON**. I grew

up in Muskegon Heights, Michigan, where there are lots of lakes and parks and beaches. My favorite color is pink and my favorite books are filled with mystery and adventure. I can't wait to share more stories with you guys, my new friends.

My name is **GLADYS JOSE**. I grew up in

Orlando, Florida, where each summer my friends and I had adventures pretending we were secret agents. Now I create art every day, with the help of my four-year-old daughter, who has taken on the role of art director, a.k.a. she tells me when I need to redraw something.